THE KELVINHILL KIDS
Visit The Kelpies

Written by Jamie Szymkowiak
Illustrated by Ali Currie

First Edition published in 2017
by Hoolet Publishing, in Glasgow, Scotland
For more information, visit hoolet.scot

ISBN: 978-0-9957548-0-5

Printed in Scotland

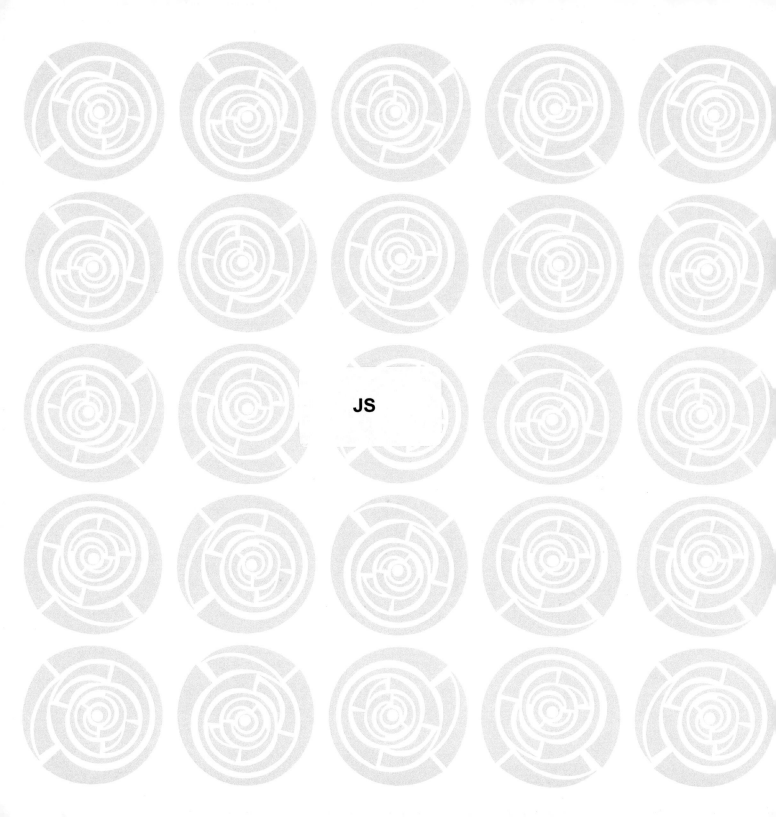

JS

THE KELVINHILL KIDS
Visit The Kelpies

For Christopher
Thanks to Dr A Abel

This book includes illustrations inspired by
the sculpture "The Kelpies" by Andy Scott.
Thank you for creating such a beautiful landmark.

It was the start of the summer holidays and Fraser wanted to go on an adventure.

"GRANNY!"

shouted Fraser, "I want to go on an adventure. Where can we go?"

"You should ask your friend Iona, she always has great ideas," replied Granny Flora, making a fresh pot of tea.
Fraser picked up the telephone to call Iona.

"IONA!"

called Mrs Innes. "Fraser's on the phone for you."
Fraser told Iona about his idea and asked where they should go.

"Let's go to The Kelpies!"
said Iona excitedly.
"My mum can drive us there
and I'll invite Grace and Hiran."

"Fraser picked a sunny day for an adventure," said Mrs Innes, helping Iona into their
BIG YELLOW CAR.

"I'm so happy it's not raining," said Iona, smiling.
"Can we go to Fraser's house first, Mum?
Hiran will be so excited to see us arrive together."

Mrs Innes' car arrived outside Hiran's house to pick him up.

"Be on your best behaviour for Mrs Innes,"
instructed Mr Harjeet, waving goodbye to his son.

"BYE DAD!" shouted Hiran.
He was very happy to see his friends.

"WE'RE HERE!"

declared an excited Iona. "Let's take a group photograph in front of The Kelpies!"
"Great idea, Iona. Granny Flora would love to see this," said Fraser, nodding in agreement.

As Mrs Innes and the kids were heading to The Kelpies, Fraser recognised someone ahead.
"Look Iona, Grace is here!" shouted Fraser.

"Grace, your friends are here too,"
said Grant, nudging his sister.

"WOOF WOOF WOOF!"

barked Gus the guide dog.

"Gus, calm down!" said Grace, as
her guide dog wagged his tail.
Walking towards The Kelpies,
Grant chuckled and said,
"Let's go meet your friends before
Gus gets us into trouble."

"Tell me what they look like," said Grace.

"THEY'RE BEAUTIFUL"

replied Iona. "Like huge shiny horses! One is looking at us and the other is watching the clouds in the sky."

"Neigh!" bellowed Hiran, as the sun bounced off the magnificent silver creatures. "We should take our photo underneath one of them," suggested Fraser, leading his friends closer to The Kelpies.

"Big smiles! Say cheese," instructed Mrs Innes.

"CHEESE!" roared the kids.

"Well done everyone," said Grant. "Shall we get some ice cream?"

Grace grinned and said, "Strawberry for me, please."

"De-lic-ious," said Grace, wiping leftovers from her face.

"I know the secret story of the Kelpies," said Iona proudly.

She looked at Hiran and whispered, "Do you want me to tell you?"

"Yes please," replied an eager Hiran.

As the kids finished their ice cream, Iona told them about

THE LEGEND OF THE KELPIES.

"The Kelpies live in the lochs of Scotland," declared Iona. "Grown-ups can't see them. They only come out from the water when they know children are near. The lochs are deep and the water is very cold. The magical Kelpies keep kids safe. They protect us."

"WOW" gasped Hiran, listening to Iona's every word.

As Iona's story came to an end,
Fraser's tummy rumbled loudly.
"It's time for us to go," said Mrs Innes.
"Granny Flora will have Fraser's dinner ready."
"SEE YOU SOON"
said Iona, waving goodbye to Grace.

"GRANNY! IT'S ME! I'M HOME!"

said Fraser, bursting through the door.

"How was your day, Fraser?" asked Granny Flora.

"Start from the very beginning and tell me all about it."

"It was brilliant," said Fraser.
"I can't wait until our next adventure."
Fraser sat on the red sofa and told
Granny Flora about his big day out.

For more information on The Kelvinhill Kids including character biographies, printable colouring pages, videos and audio, please visit www.hoolet.scot

If you enjoyed this book, you may also be interested in the world of Mini Mimi. This perfectly polite pupil is as brazen as she is bonnie. You can order Mimi's first book by visiting www.hoolet.scot